Walt Disney
Pictures Presents

The RESCUERS DOWN UNDER

Adapted by Michael Teitelbaum
Illustrated by Franc Mateu

A GOLDEN BOOK • NEW YORK
Western Publishing Company, Inc., Racine, Wisconsin 53404

MCMXCI

One morning, in the Australian countryside, Faloo the kangaroo called for her friend Cody. "Come on, Cody," Faloo shouted. "We've no time to lose!"

Eight-year-old Cody jumped from his bed, threw on his clothes, and dashed out the door. "What's going on, Faloo?" the boy asked.

"It's Marahute, the great golden eagle," answered
Faloo as the two friends raced toward a tall cliff.
"She's been caught in a poacher's net. You've got to
help set her free!"

Cody began the long climb to the cliff top. "Be
careful, Cody," warned Faloo. "Marahute doesn't
know you, so she might panic."

When Cody reached the top of the cliff, he saw Marahute stuck in a net. He started to cut her free. The eagle began to screech.

"I'm here to help," said Cody. Cody cut the net, freeing Marahute, but the great bird panicked and knocked Cody off the cliff.

"Help!" shouted Cody as he fell toward the valley below.

Marahute swooped down and caught Cody on her back, just before the boy hit the ground. Up they soared, high above the cliffs. Cody had saved Marahute, and now Marahute saved Cody.

Marahute and Cody returned to the cliff. She showed him her nest filled with eggs, and she gave Cody one of her feathers to thank him for saving her.

Cody tied the feather onto his backpack, then Marahute flew him down to the base of the cliff. Cody knew that he had made a true friend that day.

On the way home, Cody spotted a tiny mouse that was caught in a poacher's trap. As Cody tried to free the mouse both the boy and the mouse tumbled into a pit in the forest floor.

"You were just here as bait so some hunter could catch a bigger forest animal!" Cody said to the mouse.

"Well, Joanna, what have we caught today?"
boomed a voice from above. It was McLeach, the
poacher. Even though it was against the law to trap
animals in the area, McLeach had set traps all
through the forest. Joanna, his pet lizard, licked her
lips as she stared down at the mouse beside Cody. The
mouse scrambled into Cody's backpack and hid.

"Why, it's a boy!" said McLeach, reaching down to help Cody up. Then he noticed the eagle feather on Cody's pack. "Where did you get that pretty feather?" McLeach demanded.

"I can't tell you," answered Cody, who knew that McLeach would hunt Marahute down. "It's a secret!"

"Oh, it is, is it?" growled McLeach. "Well, I'm not letting you go until you tell me where the eagle is!"

As McLeach carried Cody away the little mouse leapt from Cody's pack and ran off into the forest.

The mouse soon arrived at a mouse-sized telegraph station, deep in the Australian outback. A message was sent to the Rescue Aid Society's headquarters in New York City.

At that moment its two top agents, Bianca and Bernard, were having a romantic dinner. Bernard was trying to ask Bianca to marry him.

Suddenly the two agents were interrupted and called into an emergency meeting.

"A young boy is in terrible trouble in Australia," began the chairmouse. "He needs our help!"

"Of course Bernard and I will accept the mission!" said Bianca.

"We will?" asked Bernard.

"I'm glad you agree, darling," continued Bianca. "We must leave immediately for Australia!"

Outside, a blizzard raged. When Bernard and
Bianca left headquarters and stepped out onto the
roof, they were greeted by Wilbur the albatross.
Wilbur ran Albatross Air. He was the pilot *and* the
plane.

"Albatross Air service to Australia, now boarding!"
announced Wilbur. Following a shaky takeoff, Wilbur
soared through the snowy sky, carrying Bernard and
Bianca in a sardine can strapped to his back.

When the Rescuers arrived in Australia, they were met by Jake, an Australian mouse who had found out about their mission. "Are you taking the Suicide Trail through Nightmare Canyon?" asked Jake. "Then you'll have to cross Bloodworm Creek and go through Dead Dingo Pass."

"Wait a minute!" exclaimed Bernard. "I don't see any of those places on the map!"

"Listen, mate," said Jake. "A map's no good in the outback. You've got to go on instinct. Just follow me." Soon the three mice were on their way through the outback, heading for McLeach's compound.

Meanwhile, at McLeach's compound, Cody and several animals were being held prisoner in separate cages. Red the kangaroo had been caught by McLeach, as well as Krebbs, a grumpy old koala, and Frank, a frill-necked lizard.

Frank had been trying to pick the lock on his cage with his tail. Suddenly he succeeded, and his door swung open.

"I'm free! I'm free! I'm free!" shouted Frank. But Joanna quickly burst through the door and chased Frank back into his cage.

In the next room, McLeach was hatching a plan. "I know how to get the boy to lead me to the eagle!"

Bernard, Bianca, and Jake finally finished their long trip through the outback. They arrived at McLeach's compound just in time to see McLeach throw Cody out the door.

"It's all over, boy," shouted McLeach. "Someone shot the eagle! I guess her eggs will never make it without their mother. Too bad. Now go on, get out of here!"

Cody ran off as fast as he could.

"Why is he letting Cody go?" asked Bernard.

"It's got to be a trick," answered Jake.

Then they heard McLeach talking to his pet lizard. "It worked, Joanna," said McLeach. "That boy will go right to the eggs to protect them. All we have to do is follow. Come on. Let's go!" McLeach got into his truck, a huge poaching machine called a Bushwacker.

"Jump!" shouted Jake as the Bushwacker pulled away.

"Jump?" asked Bernard.

"Jump!" Jake said again. "Onto the truck. It's the only chance we have of saving Cody and the eagle!" The three mice jumped onto the back of McLeach's truck as it sped away after Cody.

Soon Cody arrived at the cliff. He climbed down to
Marahute's nest. "I've got to save the eggs!" he
thought. Suddenly the great golden eagle appeared in
the sky. "Marahute! You're alive!" shouted Cody
happily.

At that moment, McLeach's truck stopped at the
edge of the cliff. The Rescuers leapt off and scurried
down to the eagle's nest. "Cody, you must listen to
me," began Bianca. "It's a trap."

Suddenly a shot rang out.

"Look out, Marahute!" screamed Cody, but it was too late. McLeach had shot a net into the air and it now covered Marahute, trapping the eagle. As the captured eagle swung toward them Cody, Bianca, and Jake jumped onto the net and were pulled up into McLeach's truck.

Bernard's jump had missed, so he could only watch as McLeach captured his friends and put them into a cage in the truck. When the Bushwacker sped off, Bernard hurried after it.

When McLeach arrived at Crocodile Falls, he kept Marahute locked in the cage while he dangled Cody by a rope over the water. A crane on the truck lowered the boy down toward a river full of hungry crocodiles.

"I've got to do something fast," thought Bernard, who had finally caught up with the others.

Just as Cody was about to hit the water Bernard turned the power off on the crane. Cody dangled inches above the hungry crocs.

"Hey!" shouted McLeach. "Who stole the keys?"

Bernard threw the keys to Bianca and Jake so they could set themselves and Marahute free. Then Joanna began to chase Bernard toward the river, where McLeach stood.

Bernard ran right through McLeach's legs. When Joanna tried to follow, she knocked them all over the edge and into the river, where the current carried them away downstream.

"Help!" cried Cody. The rope holding Cody snapped, and the boy plunged into the river.

Marahute swooped down, with Jake and Bianca riding on her back. She pulled Cody and Bernard from the river and brought them up to safety.

"Oh, Bernard, you are absolutely the hero of the day!" cried Bianca.

"Miss Bianca," blurted Bernard before anything else could happen. "Will you marry me?"

"Why, Bernard, of course!" answered Bianca. "And we'll invite all of our Australian friends to the wedding!"